THE Big Green Pocketbook

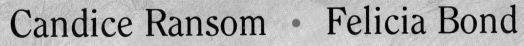

Candice Ransom • Felicia Bond

A Laura Geringer Book

An Imprint of HarperCollinsPublishers

Library of Congress Cataloging-in-Publication Data
Ransom, Candice F., date
 The big green pocketbook / by Candice Ransom ; illustrated by
Felicia Bond.
  p.   cm.
 "A Laura Geringer book."
 Summary: A little girl fills the pocketbook she carries with
mementos of the places she and her mother visit when they go
to town.
 ISBN 0-06-020848-1. — ISBN 0-06-020849-X (lib. bdg.)
 ISBN 0-06-443395-1 (pbk.)
 [1. City and town life—Fiction. 2. Mothers and daughters—
Fiction. 3. Handbags—Fiction.] I. Bond, Felicia, ill.
II. Title.
PZ7.R1743Bi   1993
[E]—dc20   92-29393
                                             CIP
                                             AC

For my mother,
who gave me the big green pocketbook
and filled it full of stories

C.F.R.

For Ellen and Anne

F.B.

This morning Mama and I are taking the bus to town. Mama hooks her big blue pocketbook over her arm. She tells me to hurry, or we will miss the bus. I get my big green pocketbook that's just like Mama's. Only, mine is empty. I can't think of anything to put in it, and Mama says, "Hurry!"

We wait for the bus at the end of our driveway. Cars pop over the hill. They look like pick-up ducks at the fair. Mama stands ready to flag the bus, but I see it first. I wave my big green pocketbook.

A hot cloud comes out of the bus. I hold my breath as we climb on. Mama lets me drop money into the box. The bus driver gives me some punched tickets. I put them in my pocketbook.

"That's a great pocketbook," he says. When he leans over to close the door, his leather seat creaks.

We go to the bank. The cool marble walls smell like pennies.
"My, what a big purse," says the bank teller. She stamps my
mother's papers, *ker-chunk, ker-chunk.*

Then she hands me two lollipops, yellow and purple. "One for now and one for later."

I put the purple one in my pocketbook.

Next we go to the insurance office. There is an umbrella painted on the door. Mama fills out some forms. The secretary lets me sit at her typewriter. I type my name, first in big letters, then in little letters.

Mama wants to go to the jewelry store. I stare
at the rings in the glass cases. The stones are all
the colors of the rainbow.

"A pocketbook that big," the jewelry man says,
"must belong to someone important."

The jewelry man gives me a key chain. I don't
have any keys, but it clinks when I put it in my
pocketbook.

We go to the dry cleaner's. The machine with shirts and dresses in plastic bags winds around and around. I would like to ride on it. Like magic, it stops at Mama's suit. The dry cleaner lady taps my pocketbook.

"What a pretty shade of green," she says. She gives me a tiny calendar.

The inside of the five-and-ten store is dim. My shoes clump on the wooden floors. Mama buys some flowered material and a pack of sewing needles. Then we look for a present for Daddy. We get a sack of gumdrops shaped like orange slices.

The candy lady says, "Fine day for you ladies to be out and about."

That makes me giggle. "She called us ladies!"

99¢

My pocketbook is starting to get full.

Our last stop is the drugstore. Mama buys a hot-water bottle. She gives me money to buy a new box of crayons. We have ice cream at the soda counter. The scoops of ice cream are square and come in a chilled silver dish. I click the spoon against my teeth and twirl my stool.

The bus picks us up in front of the drugstore. I show the driver all the things in my pocketbook.

On the ride home, I'm sleepy.

"Wake up," Mama says in a faraway voice. "We're here."

I help her gather up all her packages, and we climb off. The door hisses shut. Then the bus is gone in a cloud of brown smoke.

After lunch, I want to color with my new crayons. But I can't find my big green pocketbook.

"You must have left it on the bus," Mama says.

My pocketbook is gone!

Mama says, "Don't worry. You can have my straw purse."
But I don't want her straw purse. I want my big green
pocketbook. My whole morning is in my big green
pocketbook, and now it's lost.

Then I hear the bus going down the road, back to the
bus station. I run down our driveway. The red flag is
raised on our mailbox.

And there inside is my big green pocketbook! The bus driver
toots his horn at me.

That night I make two drawings with my new crayons.

One is for Mama. And the other...

is for the bus driver.